ideals
FIRESIDE ISSUE

HOME
SWEET
HOME

Dear Reader:

We hope that you will enjoy each and every page of *FIRESIDE IDEALS*. Beginning with this issue is a new feature called the Ideals Best-Loved Poets. A different poet will be presented in each issue, beginning with Grace Noll Crowell.

Because many of you have requested the reprinting of your favorite pages, we plan to feature in each issue Ideals Pages from the Past. We would like to feature your favorite poet—and those pages of past issues which remain in your memory. Please let us know your favorites.

Also, won't you help us share with your friends the inspiration and beauty they will find in Ideals publications by sending us (c/o Dept. Ed.) their names and addresses. We will send them our latest brochure featuring Ideals books and products.

We know you will like and enjoy the wonderful issues we have planned for 1978 and we will look forward to receiving your letter giving us the names and addresses of friends who will share your enthusiasm for "America's Most Beautiful and Wholesome Publications." We'll be waiting to hear from you.

Sincerely,

Ralph Luedtke
Managing Editor

Managing Editor, Ralph Luedtke
Associate Editor, Robin Lee Dennison
Photographic Editor, Gerald Koser
Production Editor, Stuart L. Zyduck

Winter Tapestry

Look out upon the hills and see
The pines in all their majesty
Bedecked in robes of ermine white
Against the chill of winter night.

Beyond the pasture in the snow
Are patterns where the wildlings go,
Huddled close and warm within
Hollow log and hedgerow trim.

Round the corner of the mill,
A winding stream of crystal still
Murmurs softly, trickles slow,
Ice stitched to the banks of snow.

Look with delight on winter's reign,
Where neath a fluffy counterpane,
Knitted by the swirling snows,
Earth claims her hour of sweet repose.

Mildred L. Jarrell

ISBN 0-89542-312-X

IDEALS—Vol. 35, No. 1—January 1978. Published bimonthly by IDEALS PUBLISHING CORP., 11315 Watertown Plank Road, Milwaukee, Wis. 53226
Second-class postage paid at Milwaukee, Wisconsin. © 1977 by IDEALS PUBLISHING CORP.
All rights reserved. Title IDEALS registered U.S. Patent Office.

ONE YEAR SUBSCRIPTION—six consecutive issues as published—only $10.00
TWO YEAR SUBSCRIPTION—twelve consecutive issues as published—only $17.00
SINGLE ISSUES—only $2.50

Photo opposite
WINTER IN IDAHO
Freelance Photographers Guild

Jack Frost

Once again old Jack Frost
And all his helpers, too,
Are busy painting windowpanes
With frosty winter view.

When I awoke this morning,
It was like a fairyland,
To see the lovely scenes
They drew with patient hand.

The beautiful designs they left,
Enchanting to behold,
Sparkled like a field of gems,
More precious than pure gold.

I marveled at the magic spell
They seemed to cast for me,
Frosty art upon the panes
Held a happy memory.

I thought of all the winter fun
I had known long ago,
Our pond of ice, our forts, the slides,
The men we built of snow.

I thank Jack Frost for frosty scenes,
Upon the windowpane,
That brought back joyful memories
Of childhood once again.

LaVerne P. Larson

a sparrow sang

A sparrow sang forth from behind the delicate drapes of darkness. His song echoed among the stars. Then he began to sing again. He held long to one plaintive note and ended with the strain incomplete, as though he could recall no more of it.

His is the voice and the manner of mystery. One cannot tell from whence his singing comes, or indeed if it is not the voice of night itself.

He speaks the language of the dreamer who has glimpsed a higher truth. He lives, thinks, and sings in poetry—being "in the world but not of it." The silver tones he breathes into solitude drip with mysticism. He chants the truth of the unbelievable; and in the magic of his voice the forest becomes peopled with fairies and sprites of heavenly order.

Sam Campbell

Painting opposite
Harry Moeller

Pototschnik

Small Town

The town was quietly nestled there
So peaceful and so small,
No great white way, no taxicabs,
No buildings grand and tall.

And yet it offered many things
That cities fail to give,
A smile, a nod, a helping hand,
A friendly way to live.

A small town where its people
Are working side by side,
Where "Love Thy Neighbor's" not a phrase,
It's lived—personified.

And though it's called a small town
It is somehow set apart,
For it's large in thought, in word, in deed
And very big at heart.

Jean Holmes

Snow on the Farm

The willow near the barnyard
Is standing staunch and still.
Snow mantles all the countryside;
And from my windowsill,

I see the split-rail fences
That punctuate the land.
They stand like white-haired sentries
And with an air so grand!

The cow path lost to sight now,
The old pump straight and tall,
Stand now as muted evidence
As snow covers it all!

We've made tracks to the woodshed,
And to the barnyard, too;
The countryside in winter
Affords a thrilling view!

Georgia B. Adams

Photo opposite
EAST HAMPTON, CONN.
Fred M. Dole

Winter Evenings

Winter evenings at our house
When the snow was blowing round,
Drifting high along the fence
Or piling up a mound
Between the barn and corncrib,
And changing every form
Of post or shed or bush and tree,
Our house inside was warm.

The hickory wood was crackling
As it burned inside the stove,
And the kitchen where we lived the most
Became a sheltered cove.
The wind was fiercely blowing
As the blizzard raged outside;
But in the kitchen calmly,
We the winter wind defied.

A basketful of apples
Dug from out the apple hill,
Red and green, some striped, too,
I see and taste them still.
Old Shep, the dog's behind the stove,
Stretched out and sound asleep,
While the cat purrs on the woodbox,
As she washes up her feet.

But time has made its changes,
And those days, forever past,
Are only just a memory, dear,
We hope will ever last
To help us in these modern days
As here and there we roam;
See after all, there's no place quite
As dear as home, sweet home.

Ottis Shirk

Home Indeed

Draw up a chair and light a light
And find a book to read.
The heavens are dark, and wild the night,
And home is home indeed.
The louder seems the winter's ire
Tonight, the brighter seems the fire;
For when the wintry storms begin,
The more the comfort here within.

The wind is at the windowpane,
The wind is at the door;
It shakes the house and shakes in vain,
For loud the chimney's roar.
And higher leaps the crimson blaze
In winter than in summer days;
The more the weather is unkind,
A greater joy within we find.

The fields in springtime call us forth,
Their rosy paths to roam;
But when the wind is in the north,
We pluck the rose at home.
Perhaps God sends the wintry hours
To show that there are other flowers;
For when a roof and fire you need,
Ah, then a home is home indeed!

Douglas Malloch

Wanderer

I wish I could go where the breezes go,
  Dancing and frolicking to and fro;
Wandering off to some foreign land,
  Skipping around in the desert sand.

Whipping up whitecaps, pushing a sail,
  Refreshing a hiker along a trail;
Curling in nooks and crannies with ease,
  I could go wherever I please.

And then, before I'd cease to roam,
  For an encore, as I headed home,
I'd touch a mountain, capped with snow;
  If I could go where the breezes go.

Marilyn Ellena

The Skating Pond

As I sit here reminiscing
 about days of long ago,
I can almost hear the northern winds
 and see the drifting snow.
And if I close my eyelids,
 a picture comes to mind
Of skating ponds and childhood friends;
 and as my thoughts unwind,
I hear again our laughter
 as we glided o'er the ice
And even hear the dinner gong
 as it rings first once, then twice,
Calling all the skaters
 to warm beside the fire,

Sipping hot chocolate and telling tales
 as the embers slowly expire.
A mound of mittens on the floor,
 a row of hanging skates,
Red scarfs and hats and jackets,
 chunks of cake on china plates,
The aroma of woodsmoke in the room,
 kerosene lamps, soft light,
And finally, childish voices,
 echoing songs into the night,
And then it all was over;
 and we turned our faces toward home
With a memory tucked inside our hearts
 to recall whenever we'd roam.

Shirley Sallay

JAY KILLIAN

Maple Memories

Country roads have much to offer,
   Snowmobiling's very fine,
But my heart sees sugar maples
   Standing proudly in a line.

Rugged lanes spread out before us,
   Riding snugly in our car,
Memory turns to Dad's old bobsled,
   Gathering sap in pail and jar.

Country towns bid tourists welcome;
   How we love their simple ways.
I remember helping Mother
   Build an old sap-boiling blaze.

Antiques now are all the fashion,
   Passing years are all it takes.
Strange, they remind me of my childhood–
   Little molds for sugar cakes.

Country roads are fun to travel.
   That's where recollections start.
Though the snow is deep and frosty,
   Maple memories warm the heart.

Alice Leedy Mason

Photo opposite
MAPLE SUGARING
NORTH CONWAY, NEW HAMPSHIRE
Dick Smith

Sojourn

The fire's glowing in the grate;
Let's have a cup of tea,
And draw our chairs up to the hearth
And share a memory.

The open fire gives a warmth
Like that between two friends;
Together we'll enjoy the logs
Before the evening ends.

A fireside is meant to share,
Like books and dreams and views;
This room becomes much cozier
When you are in it too.

Virginia Covey Boswell

Fireside Friends

Welcome, friend. Give me your wrap,
Please stay a little while . . .
And, when you go, leave me a bit
Of sunshine from your smile.

While we chat I'll make some tea,
And long before we part
I'll share the warmth and fellowship
Of love within your heart.

And when you must go on your way
Your memory will shine,
And music of your laughter lift
This thankful heart of mine.

D. A. Hoover

Snow Night

This night is like a precious gift
   When all is blanketed with snow;
It's time for sitting by the fire
   And reading in the soft lamp glow.

The world is hushed as nature takes
   A quiet rest and winter sleep;
The woodlands dream their tranquil dreams;
   The silvered streams are frozen deep.

The soul refreshes from the calm
   When earth is white and hurries cease;
Contentment spreads its silken wings;
   Hearts find a sweet accord with peace.

Inez Franck

Winter's Friendliness

Gray wisps of smoke from the chimney
   spiraling to the sky;
Golden candles in the windows
   welcoming passersby.

Touches of warmth and friendliness,
   logfire and candleglow,
Lend magical charm to winter
   this wondrous night of snow.

Vera Hardman

from the
editor's scrapbook

There is no such thing as bad weather; the good Lord simply sends us different kinds of good weather.

John Ruskin

A house is built of logs and stone,
Of tiles and posts and piers;
A home is built of loving deeds
That stand a thousand years.

Victor Hugo

Winter's the time for woody smoke,
Bare the branch of every oak;
White is the snow for miles around;
Winter's the time for quiet sound.

Martin Buxbaum

There are quiet hours and lonely hours,
And hours that have no end;
But the wonderful hour is the evening hour,
When you walk beside a friend.

Author Unknown

A warm smile is an invitation to draw up a chair before the log fire of friendship.

Author Unknown

Look well to the hearthstone; therein all hope for America lies.

Calvin Coolidge

The spirit of a household reaches farther than from the front door to the back. It shines forth from a child's eyes and shows in the way a man hurries back to his home.

Author Unknown

O the snow, the beautiful snow,
Filling the sky and earth below,
Over the housetops, over the street,
Over the heads of the people you meet,
Dancing, flirting, skimming along.

James W. Watson

Sweet is the smile of home; the mutual look, when hearts are of each other sure.

John Keble

We live in a wonderful world that is full of beauty, and charm, and adventure. There is no end to the adventures that we can have if only we seek them with our eyes open.

Nehru

The smoke ascends to heaven as lightly from a cottage hearth as from the haughty palace. He whose soul ponders this true equality may walk the fields of earth with gratitude and hope.

William Wordsworth

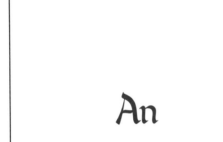

An Old-Fashioned Winter

As children, we would gather round
The hearthfire and its cheerful glow
And listen to the crackling sound
Of burning logs, with lamps turned low.
We'd gaze wide-eyed into the fire,
Delaying when we had to go
To chilly bedroom to retire,
For the fire warmed us so.

But in our featherbeds so light,
With hot wrapped irons at our feet,
We'd sleep all through the blustery night,
Oblivious of the snow and sleet.
At daybreak when the sun would peep
Through shuttered window old and worn,
Out of our cozy beds we'd creep
To view the scene left by the storm.

Elsie Natalie Brady

Painting opposite
THE QUIET HOUR
John Slobodnik

Grace Noll Crowell

Long a favorite poet in America, Grace Noll Crowell was born in 1877 in Inland, Iowa. A childhood spent on the farm instilled in her a love of nature and provided material for the rural imagery reflected in so many of her works. She married Norman H. Crowell in 1901 and settled in Texas. After her first poem was published in 1906, she wrote over 5,000 additional poems and published more than forty volumes. Although she died in 1961, her beautiful lyrical poetry, setting forth the ideas of hope and inspiration, continues to make her a much beloved poet in America and in the many other countries where her work appears. On these two pages are just a few of the many poems written by this noted poet.

There is no Desolation

Trees bare of leaves are never bare of beauty.
God made it that no thing be desolate:
Low dunes along a wind-swept sea at evening,
Glow out like scarlet embers in a grate.
The leafless, tawny reaches of old deserts
Hold every changing color of the dawn;
A strange insistent loveliness clings mutely
To jewel-knuckled weeds when life is gone.

Oh, singers of all loveliness, remember
The unsung splendor of each barren thing.
So long as hearts need comfort there is beauty;
There will be songs while there is need to sing.
And we will seek white stars above the darkness;
The sun beyond the shadows deep and long,
And we will climb the stars on slim bright ladders
To build high places on the peaks of song.

Pigeons in the Snow

Fluttering birds through the falling snow,
Softly their whirring wing-tips throw
A flurry of white flakes, shattering
Their tremulous slant, and scattering
A frost-dust as they wheel and light
Like feather flowers, dusky white
And slaty gray, and buff and brown,
Circling, swooping, coming down
A mist of color on the day,
A snow-veiled, heavenly bouquet
That falls and takes my breath away.

The Day

"The day will bring some lovely thing,"
I say it over each new dawn:
"Some gay, adventurous thing to hold
Against my heart when it is gone,"
And so I rise and go to meet
The day with wings upon my feet.

I come upon it unaware;
Some sudden beauty without name:
A snatch of song, a breath of pine,
A poem lit with golden flame;
High tangled bird notes, keenly thinned,
Like flying color on the wind.

No day has ever failed me quite:
Before the grayest day is done
I find some misty purple bloom,
Or a late line of crimson sun.
Each night I pause —remembering—
Some gay, adventurous, lovely thing.

A Wintry Mile

Walk a mile in the winter twilight,
Mark its whiteness and breathe its cold,
Reach your hand to the sunset embers,
Warm them there, and when you are old
There will be times when you will recall it:
A beautiful, perfect, shining while,
That will glow in your heart
Like a splendid diamond—
You will remember that winter mile.

You will recall the clean, cold stinging
Of winter wind on your throat and lips;
The lift of your heart in its youthful gladness,
The tingle of blood to your fingertips;
You will have drawn to your heart forever
This hour, the snow, the light in the west—
Walk awhile in the winter twilight,
Store its treasures within your breast.

MY WINDOW GARDEN

I keep upon my windowsill
  A breath of summer air;
Though the snow is falling,
  A hint of spring is there.

A walk amid the blossoms
  Alights a gloomy day,
As frosty silver frescoes
  The once-plain panes array.

The glossy green begonias,
  The soft pastel of mums,
Still grace my window garden
  Even though winter comes.

This year there are strawberries
  (I did it just in fun)
And I shall have green peppers,
  Fresh, though summer now is done.

I think my window garden
  Well worth the work. Do you,
When winter breathes her icy breath,
  Keep a window garden, too?

Bonnie Morgan

Winter Snow

I shall neglect some trivial household task
Here by the window, in my chair, to bask;
I'll watch a million snowflakes sifting by
Without a single whisper or a sigh—
Serene and still, they settle one by one;
To lie in wait for children's winter fun.

I still remember scenes of long ago—
The thrilling sights of wondrous winter's snow.
I can remember stinging hands and toes,
And battling with that irksome, runny nose;
The rolling up of snowmen—fat and tall,
The stinging whack of some cold, icy ball.

Now let the younger generation play—
I'll thrill to winter's snow in my own way!

Anna Daisy Siemens

It seems as though chess has been with us almost since the beginning of civilization. Some experts trace its beginnings back over four thousand years to a game played in northern India by four players, each controlling eight pieces on a sixty-four-square board.

The game must have crossed from India to Egypt. At any rate, Queen Nefertiti probably enjoyed a game of chess occasionally; a painting on her tomb at Karnack portrays the queen at a chess board.

Chessmen remain a popular subject for gifts and collections. Through the centuries, artisans have crafted sets in the form of everything from Egyptian pharoahs and queens in almost sphinx-like poses to modern acrylic sets in functional cubes and cylinders of varying sizes. Modern sets range from a Dada-surrealistic set designed by Max Ernst to those fashioned by retired architect Max Gluckman from discarded pepper mills, two-ounce liquor bottles or junk kings thumbing their noses at their queens.

Those who play no chess at all still appreciate and are fascinated by the beauty and originality of chessmen. German craftsmen from the eighteenth century on have excelled in hand-carved chess pieces; artisans of the Tyrolian and Black Forest areas turned out exquisitely carved pieces set on silver bases.

England produced a chess set, however, which had the largest impact of any in the history of chess. In 1835 Nathaniel Cook designed a set to prevent the confusion which these different sets had caused. Players often had difficulty distinguishing pieces because of the artistry of the manufacturer; no common symbols for the pieces existed. Cook used the obvious symbols in his set: a crown for the king, for the queen a coronet. A castle symbolized the rook, the knight by a horse's head. Each symbol was mounted on a plain stem rising from a wide and stable base. Cook named the set for his friend and English chess master, John Staunton. For actual play, the Staunton set has never been equaled.

To many, chess is seen to be the battle of life itself on a small scale. The design of the chess pieces reflects this attitude as king faces king, and bishop sidles up to queen. The end of the game the world over is signalled by the word check-mate from *shah mat*, which translated means "the king is defeated." This facet of the game has inspired satirists the world over. In nineteenth-century France, a popular motif of chess sets was Napoleon and Josephine as king and queen facing the Duke and Duchess of Waterloo.

A potentate once asked the Caliph Haun al-Rashind, "What is chess?" The Caliph answered, "What is life?" In seventeenth-century England, the playwright Thomas Middleton mixed life and chess in a dramatic political satire on the reign of James I, titled *A Game at Chesse*. When James returned from his travels, the play closed, Middleton's career ended, and the actors were jailed.

Chess still lives, however, at Marostica in northern Italy as a ceremonial game of living chess is periodically enacted. Knights sit astride horses, ceremonial flags fly at attention, and pawns stand in anticipation as black team faces white team on a city-block sized board where the game is played to check-mate before an attentive crowd. Such is life.

Patricia Pingry

In 1887, St. Paul, Minnesota, built an ice palace large enough to hold 25,000 people and gave birth to a carnival which continues to thrive in this most northern city in a most unlikely time of year. About the time cold weather is firmly entrenched and northern residents set out to join the birds down South, citizens stormed and taken by Vulcanus Rex, the fire king. The carnival is then officially closed, Boreas leaves, and the stage is set, regrettably, for spring.

During the carnival, St. Paul offers a multitude of winter events such as ice fishing, speed skating, ice boat regattas, mutt races featuring the family pet, and

WINTER CARNIVAL

of St. Paul put on their party clothes, dig out their snowshoes, and pay homage to winter. As incredible as the idea sounds, at the end of January, they invite the world to come to their land of ice and snow for some outdoor fun.

This frozen Mardi Gras began after an Eastern writer wrote that St. Paul was "another Siberia, unfit for human habitation." Determined to show the world that Minnesotans do not hibernate for half the year, the city began to build one of the most unique festivals ever.

Festivities begin with a gala parade down snowy streets, marking the beginning of the reign of the legendary monarch of ice and snow, King Boreas, and his Queen of Snows and royal court. After ten days, the King's ice palace is

curling. Other sports also, in defiance of the ice and snow, prevail. There are car races on ice, softball on an ice diamond, and hot-air balloon races amid snow-laden clouds. For the non-sports minded, St. Paul features an ice sculpturing contest.

Today, the ice palace is considerably smaller than in 1887, some years little more than a front with a portal. The Carnival, however, and the fun and events have grown. This January, the harsh cold of the north will again settle in, and the snow and ice will return to paralyze the scene; but in St. Paul, the city will come alive and sparkle. And winter will be a little warmer because of it.

Patricia Rawles

Saint Paul Winter Carnival Ice Palace 1888

Down Country Roads

Down country roads I love to wander
  While the snow falls thick and fast,
To revel in the cold, white stillness
  Of a beauty unsurpassed!

Stomping along through trackless snowpaths,
  Past the tumbling fences, too,
I pause so often just to gather
  All the magic of the view!

Past rolling farmlands and snow-clad barns,
  Stretching to the distant hill,
The snow like a sleeping kitten lies,
  Oh, so fluffy, soft and still!

The magic of the crested woodlands
  Lures me on; and I must go
Down the country roads, just to wander
  Through the newly fallen snow!

Georgia B. Adams

Photo opposite
COUNTRY SNOWFALL
SAUK COUNTY, WIS.
Ken Dequaine

Overleaf
NEWBURY, VERMONT
Fred M. Dole

WHITE BIRCHES IN THE SNOW

Once on a starless winter's night,
Paths gone, snow pillowed everywhere,
Lost in an endless field of white,
I saw tall birches standing there.

Those lofty sentinels held ground
Where, ice enclosed, the brook was mute.
In all the world no other sound
Than wind in birch trees like a flute.

What towers of strength, what confidence
To one who sought to find the way.
Their silent vigil in another sense
Was like a beacon leading to the day.

Silver trees lifted thoughts above,
Beauty like none other that I know.
God had shown a special kind of love
To place white birches in the snow.

Aron Christopher

Photo opposite
CARSON PASS
SIERRA NEVADA MOUNTAINS
Joseph A. Barnett

Washington's Birthday

'Tis splendid to live so grandly,
   That long after you are gone,
The things you did are remembered
   And recounted under the sun;
To live so bravely and purely,
   That a nation stops on its way,
And once a year, with banner and drum,
   Keeps its thought of your natal day.

'Tis splendid to have a record,
   So white and free from stain
That held to the light it shows no blot,
   Though tested and tried amain;
That age to age forever
   Repeats its story of love,
And your birthday lives in a nation's heart,
   All other days above.

And this is Washington's glory,
   A steadfast soul and true,
Who stood for his country's honor
   When his country's days were few.
And now when its days are many,
   And its flag of stars is flung
To the breeze in defiant challenge,
   His name is on every tongue.

Yes, it's splendid to live so bravely,
   To be so great and strong,
That your memory is ever a tocsin
   To rally the foes of the wrong;
To live so proudly and purely
   That your people pause in their way,
And year by year, with banner and drum,
   Keep the thought of your natal day.

Margaret E. Sangster

Painting opposite
GEORGE WASHINGTON
Gilbert Stuart
(Photo: H. Armstrong Roberts)

Sandburg on Lincoln

Lincoln was 51 years old. With each year since he had become a grown man, his name and ways, and stories about him, had been spreading among plain people and their children. So tall and so bony, with so peculiar a slouch and so easy a saunter, so sad and so haunted-looking, so quizzical and comic, as if hiding a lantern that lighted and went out and that he lighted again—he was the Strange Friend and the Friendly Stranger. Like something out of a picture book for children—he was. His form of slumping arches and his face of gaunt sockets were a shape a Great Artist had scrawled from careless clay.

He looked like an original plan for an extra-long horse or a lean tawny buffalo, that a Changer had suddenly whisked into a man-shape. Or he met the eye as a clumsy, mystical giant that had walked out of a Chinese or Russian fairy story, or a bogy who had stumbled out of an ancient Saxon myth with a handkerchief full of presents he wanted to divide among all the children in the world.

He didn't wear clothes. Rather, clothes hung upon him as if on a rack to dry, or on a loose ladder up a windswept chimney. His clothes, to keep the chill or the sun off, seemed to whisper, "He put us on when he was thinking about something else."

He dressed any which way at times, in broadcloth, a silk hat, a silk choker, and a flaming red silk handkerchief, so that one court clerk said Lincoln was "fashionably dressed, as neatly attired as any lawyer at court, except Ward Lamon." Or again, people said Lincoln looked like a huge skeleton with skin over the bones, and clothes covering the skin.

The stove pipe hat he wore sort of whistled softly: "I am not a hat at all; I am the little garret roof where he tucks in little thoughts he writes on pieces of paper." The hat, size seven and one-eighth, had a brim one and three-quarters inches wide. The inside band in which the more important letters and notes were tucked, measured two and three-quarters inches. The cylinder of the stovepipe was 22 inches in circumference. The hat was lined with heavy silk and, measured inside, exactly six inches deep. And people tried to guess what was going on under that hat. Written in pencil on the imitation satin paper that formed part of the lining was the signature "A. Lincoln, Springfield, Ill.," so that any forgetful person who might take the hat by mistake would know where to bring it back. Also the hatmaker, "George Hall, Springfield, Ill.," had printed his name in the hat so that Lincoln would know where to get another one just like it.

The umbrella with the name "Abraham Lincoln" stitched in, faded and drab from many rains and regular travels, looked sleepy and murmuring. "Sometime we shall have all the sleep we want, we shall turn the law office over to the spiders and the cobwebs; and we shall quit politics for keeps."

There could have been times when children and dreamers looked at Abraham Lincoln and lazily drew their eyelids half shut and let their hearts roam about him—and they half-believed him to be a tall horse chestnut tree or a rangy horse or a big wagon or a log barn full of new-mown hay—something else or more than a man, a lawyer, a Republican candidate with principles, a prominent citizen—something spreading, elusive, and mysterious—the Strange Friend and the Friendly Stranger.

Carl Sandburg

From ABRAHAM LINCOLN: THE PRAIRIE YEARS AND THE WAR YEARS, One Volume Edition by Carl Sandburg, copyright, 1926, by Harcourt Brace Jovanovich, Inc.; copyright, 1954, by Carl Sandburg. Reprinted by permission of the publishers.

It's American

If it stands for justice,
And the right of it,
If it speaks of goodness,
And the might of it,
If there's challenge, courage, joy
And pride in it . . . It's American.

If there's a helping hand,
And words of cheer in it,
If freedom for mankind
Is very clear to it,
If hope, and faith, and love
Are very dear to it . . . It's American.

Mildred L. Jarrell

Cutter Riding

As I looked out of my window
At the softly falling snow,
Longing welled within my being
Just to cutter riding go.

Down a quiet country roadside
Or a winding narrow lane,
To the long ago of childhood
Where I'd fain return again.

I still can hear the crunching snow,
As the runners slid along,
And the jingle of the sleigh bells
Ringing out their merry song.

As the horses' steady hoofbeats,
Quickened now and then their pace,
Tiny chunks of snow would often
Join the cold wind on our face.

Guess it's only wishful thinking
As I watch the falling snow,
For the chances aren't many
That I'll cutter riding go.

But there's just no harm in dreaming;
Dreams were made for folks like me
Who can travel back in memory
To the days that used to be,

Capturing some old-time magic
From such things as falling snow,
Dreaming dreams that someday maybe
I'll a cutter riding go.

Della Doane Mockridge

Photo opposite
Alpha Photo Associates

The Snowman

One day the snowman, Sir Benjamin Buzz,
He started to melt as a snowman does.

Down ran the crown of his icicled hat,
Over his forehead; and right after that

He noticed his whiskers go lolloping by,
Along with his chin, and his collar, and tie.

Then Benjamin looked and saw that his chest
Was gliding away through his coat and his vest;

And after a little he sighed, "Ho! Hum!
There goes a finger and there goes a thumb!"

And scarce had he spoken when Benjamin felt
That both of his legs were beginning to melt;

Down they ran dribbling, bit after bit,
Like two creamy candles a sunbeam had lit.

"Alas," cried Sir Ben, "I am merely a bump!"
And the next thing he knew he sat down with a thump.

Then little by little he slipped like a sleigh,
And quietly, quietly slithered away;

And next when he noticed the spot he was on,
He looked for himself and he saw he was gone.

And that is the story of Benjamin Buzz,
Who melted one day as a snowman does.

Mildred Plew Meigs

From CHILD LIFE Magazine. Copyright 1933, 1961 by Rand McNally & Company.
Used through courtesy of Rand McNally & Company; The Saturday Evening Post and
Marion P. Ruckel.

Winter's Joy

The world is wrapped in winter's cloak
   Of soft and ermine white,
A frosty world, a magic world,
   A wintertime delight.

      As children coast upon the hill
         Their merriment rings out;
      And from the meadow pond we hear
         The skaters laugh and shout.

            While out upon our lawn, there stands
               A snowman blithe and gay,
            Born of the children's artistry
               On this glad snowy day.

      Then soon you'll see his family
         Of snow folk gathered round;
      And though they chat quite happily
         They never make a sound.

But in the house the hearth fire glows,
   And in its warmth we sing
Of the wondrous beauty of this day,
   When winter reigns as king.

Vera Hardman

The Lamplighter

My tea is nearly ready and the sun has left the sky.
It's time to take the window to see Leerie going by;
For every night at teatime and before you take your seat,
With lantern and with ladder he comes posting up the street.

Now Tom would be a driver and Maria go to sea,
And my papa's a banker and as rich as he can be;
But I, when I am stronger and can choose what I'm to do,
O Leerie, I'll go round at night and light the lamps with you!

For we are very lucky, with a lamp before the door,
And Leerie stops to light it as he lights so many more;
And oh! before you hurry by with ladder and with light,
O Leerie, see a little child and nod to him tonight!

Robert Louis Stevenson

JAY KILLIAN

The Land of Counterpane

When I was sick and lay abed,
I had two pillows at my head,
And all my toys beside me lay
To keep me happy all the day.

And sometimes for an hour or so
I watched my leaden soldiers go,
With different uniforms and drills,
Among the bedclothes, through the hills;

And sometimes sent my ships in fleets
All up and down among the sheets;
Or brought my trees and houses out,
And planted cities all about.

I was the giant great and still
That sits upon the pillow-hill,
And sees before him, dale and plain,
The pleasant land of counterpane.

Robert Louis Stevenson

H. Armstrong Roberts

Nature gives to every time and season

some beauties of its own.

Dickens

God's Promises

The world lies white, serene and still,
  From frozen brook to windswept hill,
While high above, a silver star,
  In silence spreads its light afar.

The arching sky, each spruce, and pine
  Are caught within the starlight shine;
The old familiar fades from sight
  To join the beauty of the night.

The snow falls gently all around,
  Upon this place so far from town,
Where downy bird and things that creep
  Are bedding down to rest and sleep.

They have the courage to endure
  And trust that makes them feel secure;
They have their dreams that bring again
  The simple beauty of the rain.

For birds still sing through wind and cold,
  And ducklings have this truth to hold:
In spite of snow and winter's sting,
  They know that God has promised spring!

Alice Leedy Mason

When Sister Played the Piano at the Silent "Pitcher Show"

When Sister played the piano
At the silent "pitcher show,"
Her fingers danced like raindrops
On the keys . . . so long ago.

Sometimes the show was funny
(We yelled and laughed aloud!)
And then the music chuckled
As it rippled through the crowd.

When Sister did the sad scenes,
The tune held sorrow, too;
And when the show was eerie,
Dark fear came tinkling through!

When the hero chased the villain,
Sister's fingers beat like mad
As she banged a wild crescendo
Till the good man got the bad.

The love scenes! Oh, the love scenes
As we read, "Will you be mine?"
She played a tender love song,
Soft and sweet, to match the line.

Oh, what pleasure, munching popcorn,
As we watched the "pitcher show"
And listened to the music
Of our Sister . . . long ago.

Nova Trimble Ashley

The Winter Rose

Vision of loveliness beyond compare
Like some sweet fragrant dream,
How blessed are we, that we can share
Such beauty, seldom seen.

Such sweet perfection, we relate
To some bright summer morn,
But somehow, it has been your fate,
The winter to adorn.

Sweet messenger of warmer climes
We welcome you with joy
Whose fragrant petal so enshrines
Memories of days gone by.

Harold W. Barton

Seed Catalogs

'Twill not be long before they come:
The tales of tall delphinium
And every growing lovely thing
That marks the magic of the spring.

Beside the blazing fire we'll read
The miracles of root and seed
And what new bit of beauty grows
Of pansy, peony and rose.

A thousand times have growers told
Of zinnia and marigold;
But still men read their pages through
As though the oldest charms were new.

'Tis good in fancy's realm to dwell
With phlox and Canterbury bell,
And roam, away from storms and fogs,
Among the garden catalogs.

Edgar A. Guest

Magic Catalog

How nice to have a catalog
On this cold and blustery night,
The magic of its pages
To fill my heart with sweet delight.

For while the backlog crackles
And glowing flames leap high,
I still may go where fancy leads me,
Down flowering paths neath summer skies,

And linger there amid the blooms
Of bright and sunny marigolds,
The rainbow hues of tall larkspurs
Where velvet petals now unfold.

Then pause I must, where pansies grow
And lift their faces to the sun,
That I might feel the joy and rapture
Of this hour before my dream is done.

Thank you for this catalog,
Its pages bright and gay,
For its spell of sweet enchantment
Has unveiled a lovely summer day!

Joy Belle Burgess

All these I love . . .
       From years now past,
       Old-fashioned things
       Of rare, old glass:
       A paperweight
       With winter scene,
       A hobnail plate,
       A soup tureen,
       Small flasks for oil,
       A candy dish,
       Cranberry shoes,
       A silver fish,
       A crystal bowl,
       Quaint, hand-blown birds—
       Too lovely to
       Describe with words—
       A dinner bell,
       Bright red and gold.
       Some candlesticks
       (A century old),
       A pepper mill,
       Tall amber jugs,
       A punch bowl set
       With matching mugs.

Like precious gems . . .
       They shine and glow
       On window shelves
       From row to row.
       When sunbeams touch
       These treasured things,
       The memories start—
       My heart has wings!

Sara Bren

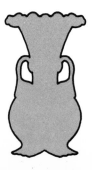

Photo opposite
CRANBERRY GLASS COLLECTION
Fred Sieb

Yesteryear

Dreaming by the fireplace
I think of yesteryear
When first I saw you smiling,
Your face so sweet and dear.

I see you by the gatepost
With snowflakes in your hair
And hear your soft voice calling
Through frosty winter air.

I hear your step come running
Along the icy path
Where I with love was waiting
Amidst the swirling wrath.

I feel your dear heart beating
As you come close to me
And kiss my cold cheek, frosty,
With shy timidity.

Yes, dreaming by my fireplace
Brings back sweet memories
When we were young, my darling,
In winter's esctacies.

Gertrude Rudberg

Little Valentine

Precious little valentine,
  with eyes all wide and blue;
Precious little girl of mine,
  so dear in all you do.
I wonder, do you know your worth,
  the love and joy you bring,
The gladness that can fill my heart
  in every song you sing.
You are Mommy's angel,
  Daddy's dream come true,
Fragrant as a rosebud,
  fresh as morning dew,
You are joys unequalled,
  all that's real and fine
Bless and keep you always,
  little valentine.

Garnett Ann Schultz

All folks want a valentine,
  and Mommy needs one, too.
Just, oh, so tall, and just so big
  with smiling eyes like you.
A darling little turned-up nose
  and freckles golden brown,
A bit of naughtiness that's sweet,
  a precious boyish frown.

All folks want a treasured kiss;
  and none's as dear to me
As when a certain "little guy"
  is perched upon my knee.
I love those tender baby arms,
  they thrill this heart of mine.
No other one can take the place
  of my "wee valentine."

Garnett Ann Schultz

Wee Valentine

*Whimsical little people opposite
made by Betty Brown
of Mequon, Wisconsin*

A Shadow for Spring

The poor little groundhog
Is down there below.
He's out of the wind
And he's out of the snow!

He's had quite a nap
Now he wants to get going!
He says, "What's the weather?
Is it raining or snowing?"

You were snug underground;
Why should you make a fuss?
You know all the answers.
Don't ask this of us!

Your public is shivering.
We're now turning blue!
Come on little groundhog,
It's all up to you!

Barbara Moran

Hungering for Spring

I have a hungering for spring,
To see the flowers grow,
And yet before tomorrow morn
I'm sure that it will snow!

I watch for robins every day,
I want to know they're here;
For we all know when robins come
That spring will soon appear!

I want the warm rain on my face,
To hear the songbirds sing,
In fact I'm tired of winter months—
I'm hungering for spring!

George L. Ehrman

Ideals' Pages
from the Past

Sweetheart

ISSUE

ideals

On the following four pages
we are presenting a selection
from Sweetheart Ideals 1954.

My Dreams Are Yours

James J. Metcalfe

Whatever dreams I ever have . . . However old or new . . . They are the pictures and the thoughts . . . I want to share with you . . . The plans I have for everything . . . I hope will come my way . . . And all the magic beauty that . . . Belongs to yesterday . . . I want to take them in my hand . . . And bring them to your door . . . And promise you that all of them . . . Are yours for evermore . . . I want your heart to understand . . . That every dream in me . . . Is one that you inspired with . . . Your love and loyalty . . . And so whatever dreams I have . . . And whether old or new . . . I want to say sincerely that . . . They all belong to you.

Beautiful Dreamer

Stephen C. Foster

Stephen C. Foster

Moderato

Beau-ti-ful dream-er, wake un-to me, Star-light and dew-drops are wait-ing for
Beau-ti-ful dream-er, out on the sea Mer-maids are chanting the wild lore-

thee; Sounds of the rude world heard in the day,
lie; O - ver the stream-let va-pors are borne,

lull'd by the moon-light have all pass'd a-way! Beau-ti-ful dream-er,
wait-ing to fade at the bright com-ing morn, Beau-ti-ful dream-er,

queen of my song, List while I woo thee with soft me-lo-dy;
beam on my heart, E'en as the morn on the streamlet and sea;

Gone are the cares of life's bu-sy throng, Beauti-ful dreamer a-wake un-to
Then will all clouds of sor-row de-part,

me! Beauti-ful dreamer a-wake un-to me!

Belief

I do not always understand
The many things I see:
The hills that climb to meet the sky,
The shore that finds the sea,
A shining star at close of day
As twilight gathers near,
And then the darkness all about
As night is quickly here.

I do not always analyze
The things before my eyes:
The mysteries too deep to know,
The hours of sweet surprise,
A stream that flows through valleys deep,
The river rushing on,
The desert sand so dry and still,
The day that's here and gone.

Belief is mine; although 'tis true
I know not how or why,
The rain shall end as it began
And sunshine light the sky.
'Tis faith alone that tells my heart
The winter too shall pass,
And spring will come to bless the world
An April day at last.

I cannot always understand
These miracles of God;
But one day all of us shall walk
The path that angels trod.
Still, I believe and always shall
In so much yet unseen;
Because a faith lives in my heart,
Belief is mine supreme.

Garnett Ann Schultz

The wintertime is bleak and cold . . . With snow and ice and sleet . . . And people always hurry when . . . They walk along the street . . . The sky is dull, the trees are bare . . . The winds are lashing gales . . . And in the darkness of the night . . . A loneliness prevails . . . But here and there the chimney-smoke . . . Appears to turn the tide . . . And there are friendly lights that shine . . . Where warmth and love abide . . . There is the comfort of a home . . . Where children laugh and play . . . And daily cares are icicles . . . That drip and melt away . . . And as the sun must rise and set . . . And boys become as men . . . The winter only lasts so long . . . And spring will come again.

James J. Metcalfe

Coming in Easter Ideals—

A series of paintings by George Hinke and Leslie Benson reflecting the Holy Season . . . Charles Wesley's beautiful hymn "Christ the Lord Is Risen Today" . . . Springtime in the Rockies with colorful photos of wild flowers . . . Easter egg customs from around the world . . . plus poetry and pictures of Easter beauty and inspiration to reflect the joyous spirit of the season.

ACKNOWLEDGMENTS

A SPARROW SANG by Sam Campbell. Copyrighted. Used with permission of Virginia M. Kerry. SEED CATALOGS by Edgar A. Guest. Copyrighted and used by permission of Washington Star Syndicate, Inc. WEE VALENTINE by Garnett Ann Schultz. From SOMETHING BEAUTIFUL by Garnett Ann Schultz. Copyright © 1966 by Garnett Ann Schultz. Published by Dorrance & Company. WINTER SNOW by Anna Daisy Siemens. From STAND TALL by Anna Daisy Siemens. Copyright © 1970 by Anna Daisy Siemens. Published by Dorrance & Company. THE LAMPLIGHTER and THE LAND OF COUNTERPANE by Robert Louis Stevenson from A CHILD'S GARDEN OF VERSES (Charles Scribner's Sons 1917).

Statement of ownership, management and circulation (Required by 39 U.S.C. 3685), of IDEALS, published bimonthly at Milwaukee, Wisconsin for September 1977. Publisher, Ideals Publishing Corporation; Managing Editor, Ralph Luedtke; Owner, Harlequin Enterprises BV, Prinsengracht 778, Amsterdam, The Netherlands 1002. The known bondholders, mortgagees, and other security holders owning or holding 1 percent or more of total amount of bonds, mortgages or other securities are: None. Average no. copies each issue during preceding 12 months: Total no. copies printed (net press run) 241,645. Paid circulation 66,392. Mail subscriptions 152,060. Total paid circulation 218,452. Free distribution 400. Total distribution 218,852. Single issue nearest to filing date: Total no. copies printed (net press run) 195,894. Paid circulation 21,834. Other sales 148,695. Free distribution 400. Total distribution 170,929. I certify that the statements made by me above are correct and complete.

James F. Cape, President.

Inside covers: Freelance Photographers Guild

Cookbooks By Ideals contain taste-tempting, mouth-watering recipes to tease the palate and delight the diner. From the very special recipes you will want to try for that elegant dinner to the simple, quick and easy to prepare, yet sure to please recipe, you will find a wide selection in each of these cookbooks. These are common-sense recipes for outstanding dishes. You need no unusual or rare ingredients. With reasonable effort and "off the shelf" ingredients you can be sure of high praise for the attractive and tasty dishes you set before your family or fortunate guests. We have added the IDEALS touch of beautiful full color photographs featuring finished dishes, with a bit of poetry and artwork to delight the cook. All books measure a full 8½" x 11" and all softcover books are beautifully bound in high gloss, easily cleaned, laminated covers. Ideals cookbooks — a pleasure to use . . . a joy to give.

Ideals Complete Family—Hardcover—112 Pages—$3.95
Sophie Kay's Family—Softcover—80 Pages—$2.50

Festive Party, Soups For All Seasons, Junior Chef,
All Holiday, Dessert, Country Kitchen, Gourmet,
Softcover — 64 Pages — $2.25 Each . . . All Others $1.95 Each

SPECIAL OFFER — SAVE UP TO $2.25
YOUR CHOICE, ANY 5 FOR $9.00
Complete Family and Sophie Kay's not included

Book Viewer Stand — This modern see-thru book stand, made of strong, durable Lucite, completely protects cookbooks and other display items from smudges and dirt. The stand conveniently folds flat for easy storage or hanging. It's perfect for use in the kitchen, workshop or home-study. Only $4.00

To order –
see COOKBOOKS section on order blank

Booklet 1

Booklet 2

New Recipe Card Booklets — Bound to be Convenient
Unlike other bulky packages of recipe cards, the Ideals Recipe Card Booklets allow homemakers to remove one perforated card at a time and what remains is a handy collection of artistically designed cards conveniently bound into one easy-to-store booklet. No more loose cards floating around in kitchen drawers — no more mixed files of used and unused cards. Each booklet contains 32 individual 3" x 5" recipe cards, plus a delightful poem and easy-to-make recipe. Two distinctive designs — Only $1.00 each

Prose
Pictures
$3.75

Proverbs
Pictures
$3.75

Prose
Pictures
$3.50

Poetry
Pictures
$3.75

Prose
Pictures
$3.75

Poetry
Pictures
$3.75

Prose
Pictures
$3.75

Poetry-Prose
Pictures
$3.75

Gift-Sized Hardbounds are specially designed with giving in mind. Each colorful book contains messages of beauty, warmth and wisdom . . . all presented in the popular 7" x 9⁷/₈" designer gift size. Among the charming stories, poems and anecdotes contained in the respective titles, full page color photos are included depicting some of life's most beautiful and rewarding inspirational experiences and sights. Here are your guides into enriching moments for yourself and for those special people who you will want to remember with selected gift copies. Turn any occasion into a special occasion . . . give an Ideals Gift-Sized hardbound. *All Books – 64 Pages*

Children's Books . . . for rainy days and stormy nights . . . for bedtime, playtime, anytime. Cuddle up with the little ones and an Ideals storybook and share some very precious times together that you and the children or grandchildren will remember and treasure forever. Children's books by Ideals feature vividly colored artwork by master illustrators in combination with traditional and contemporary tales of fun and fantasy in rhyme and story. The activity books include "think 'n' do" games, puzzles, crafts and art. Ideals children's books make memories to grow on.

Artwork
Story
32 Pages
$1.25

Artwork
Story
32 Pages
$1.25

Artwork
Story
32 Pages
$1.25

**Both Hardcover
All Others Softcover**

Story-Verse
Artwork
80 Pages
$3.00

Story-Verse
Artwork
80 Pages
$3.50

Prose
Pictures
64 Pages
$1.75

Artwork
Story
32 Pages
$1.25

Artwork
Story-Rhyme
32 Pages
$1.25

Share The Beauty & Inspiration Of IDEALS Magazine

Here is the story of the real America, the good-news stories of down-to-earth Americans and the solid ideas and ideals they live by. Each issue of IDEALS includes a beautiful collection of full color photos— nature, people, homes, interiors, antiques—art reproductions that almost jump off the page, poetry, unusual stories and articles, and stories in pictures of the almost forgotten crafts of yesterday.

IDEALS is much more than a magazine . . . it's a delightful visit with the people who have made our country great—a renewed statement of faith in the customs, beliefs and purposes of yesterday. With each issue of IDEALS, keyed to the season, you discover anew the wonderful world of our fathers, of their regard for one another, of the honesty and love and steadfast belief in the good life.

There's color, pages and pages of glorious color scenes from all over America and around the world—the kind of photos you will want to frame and keep forever for sheer pleasure. But IDEALS is much more than a beautiful magazine. It's filled with stories and verse about the things and people and customs that have made our country great. It tells about the purposes and beliefs and daily lives of good people everywhere.

OUR NEXT DELIGHTFUL ISSUE

EASTER IDEALS

with its colorful portrayal of nature's awakening to spring and its pages of enriching poetry, prose and pictures is sure to please you in all the ways you have come to know and expect from IDEALS. Think how much your friends look for, and value these same wholesome, rewarding things that have become such an important part of your life . . . and what a cherished gift a subscription to IDEALS would be for them. A gift subscription to IDEALS, starting with our colorful EASTER IDEALS, would surely brighten their holiday, as well as the rest of their year.

And as you have come to know, every bimonthly issue of IDEALS will bring more surprises and stories they'll want to save. It will soon become that same good friend and companion it has become to you.

We are so sure you and your friends will feel this way about IDEALS that we proudly extend to every new subscriber our personal

MONEY BACK GUARANTEE

If, after receiving the first copy on your subscription, you find IDEALS is not as beautiful and inspiring as you expected, just return your copy to us in its original wrapper marked "return to sender." We will cancel your subscription and the invoice due.

So share your faith in country, home and the American way of life through the beautiful pages of IDEALS — enter your gift subscriptions today! You needn't send any money now unless you prefer. Simply mark the proper area on the order blank and we'll bill you later.

IDEALS SUBSCRIPTION PLANS

ONE YEAR........6 issues as published $10.00
  (A saving of $5.00 under the single copy rate.)

TWO YEAR........12 issues as published....................$17.00
  (A saving of $13.00 under the single copy rate.)

THREE YEAR........18 issues as published.................$24.00
  (A saving of $21.00 under the single copy rate.)

4 VOLUME........4 issues as published ....$ 7.50
  (A saving of $2.50 under the single copy rate.)

PAY AS YOU READ PLAN

Use the Pay-As-You-Read Plan: 1. Send no money now. 2. Expect the current issue, or any title you designate, by return mail, with an invoice and return envelope. 3. Remit $2.00 by return mail. 4. The next issue will be sent automatically; you needn't reorder each time. If you want to cancel your pay-as-you-read subscription, notify us at least three weeks before publication date.

IDEALS
1978 PUBLICATION SCHEDULE

Fireside Ideals... Jan.
Easter Ideals... Mar.
Neighborly Ideals .... May
Countryside Ideals.. July
Thanksgiving Ideals .... Sept.
Christmas Ideals .... Nov.

"Bound To Be Beautiful"
IDEALS BINDER

As rich looking as the six issues it holds with metal rods that eliminate punching. Stiff royal blue leather-cloth cover, embossed in gold. Yours for only $4.00. Hardcover 8½ x 11 inches.

My Personal Order

YOUR NAME

ADDRESS

CITY ( )

STATE ZIP CODE

IMPORTANT MESSAGE TO OUR CUSTOMERS RE: POSTAGE*

USA
1. **ORDERS UNDER $5.00 ADD** $ .75
2. **SUBSCRIPTIONS:** **NO CHARGE**
3. **ALL GIFT BOOKS ADD** $ .10 per gift name

OUTSIDE USA
1. **ORDERS UNDER $5.00 ADD** $1.00
2. **SUBSCRIPTIONS ADD** $1.00 per sub. year
3. **ALL GIFT BOOKS ADD** $ .15 per gift name **SUBSCRIPTION YEAR**

MY IDEALS SUBSCRIPTION PLANS (FOR GIFT SUBSCRIPTIONS SEE OTHER SIDE)

1 YEAR SUBSCRIPTION $10.00	**2 YEAR SUBSCRIPTION $17.00**	**3 YEAR SUBSCRIPTION $24.00**
1-4 additional gift subs $9.00, or a total of 5 or more additional subs $8.50 ea.	1-4 additional gift subs $15.00, or a total of 5 or more additional subs $14.50 ea.	1-4 additional gift subs $21.50, or a total of 5 or more additional subs $20.50 ea.

Begin my subscription with ☐ FIRESIDE ☐ EASTER (MAR)

PAY AS YOU READ PLAN 1 copy each issue with **INVOICE** @ $2.00 (indicate beginning issue above)

COUNTRY SCENE QUARTERLY SUBSCRIPTION (4 issues) @ **$7.50** begin Country Scene ☐ Vol. 2 #4 ☐ Vol. 3 #1 (MAR)

BEAUTIFUL IDEALS ISSUES 8½ x 11 (*SPECIAL—ANY 3 FOR $6.50)—COUNTRY SCENE ISSUES 8½ x 11

QTY.	TITLE	PRICE	QTY.	TITLE	PRICE	QTY.	TITLE	PRICE
	FIRESIDE	2.50		HAPPINESS*	2.50		COUNTRY SCENE VOL. 2 #2	2.50
	EASTER (MAR)	2.50		INSPIRATION*	2.50		COUNTRY SCENE VOL. 2 #3	2.50
	NEIGHBORLY (MAY)	2.50		MEMORY*	2.50		**COUNTRY SCENE VOL. 2 #4**	2.50
	COUNTRY SIDE (JULY)	2.50		ADVENTURE*	2.50		**COUNTRY SCENE VOL. 3 #1 (MAR)**	2.50
	WOODLAND*	2.50		IDEALS BINDER (HOLDS 6 ISSUES)	4.00			

HARDBOUND ISSUES (A = 8½ x 11, B = 11 x 8½, C = 7 x 9⅞, D = 5⅞ x 7½, E = 5⅜ x 7¼ Puff cover, F = 6 x 9)

TITLE		PRICE	TITLE		PRICE	TITLE		PRICE
BECAUSE YOU ARE MY FRIEND	B	5.00	IN THE FOOTSTEPS OF THE MASTER	A	3.95	MESSAGES OF BEAUTY		
FAMOUS AMERICAN—			THE AMERICAN ALBUM	A	3.95	(WAYSIDE FLOWERS)	C	3.75
COMPOSERS	A	3.95	THE JOYS OF HOMETOWN LIVING	A	3.95	UNTIL THE RACE IS WON	A	3.75
HOUSES OF WORSHIP	A	3.95	HE LEADETH ME	A	3.95	COUNT ONLY THE SUNNY HOURS	A	3.75
THE GLORY OF EASTER	A	3.95	WOODLAND PORTRAITS	A	3.95	LET'S BE FRIENDS	C	3.50
IN THE BEGINNING	A	3.95	GOD'S CORNER	A	3.95	THE PASSING SCENE	B	3.50
NOT BY BREAD ALONE	A	3.95	A MOTHER IS LOVE	C	3.95	MOMENTS TO TREASURE	A	3.50
LETTERS OF INSPIRATION	A	3.95	PROVERBS TO LIVE BY	C	3.75	SCRAPBOOK FAVORITES	A	2.95
SEASON OF GOLD	A	3.95	THE SIMPLE JOYS	C	3.75	**WILDERNESS REFLECTIONS**	F	2.95
WINGS UPON THE HEAVENS	A	3.95	HAPPINESS IS SHARING	C	3.75	I FOUND GOD (PUFF DELUX COVER)	E	2.50
BEST LOVED POEMS FROM IDEALS	A	3.95	GOD'S PROMISES	C	3.75	**MESSAGES OF HOPE (PUFF DELUX)**	E	2.50
COMFORTING MOMENTS—			FROM THE EDITOR'S SCRAPBOOK	C	3.75	**ESP. FOR MOTHER (PUFF DELUX)**	E	2.50
THROUGH PRAYER	A	3.95						

IDEALS COOKBOOKS (SOFT COVER) 8½ x 11 — *HARDBOUND (SPECIAL ANY 5 FOR $9.00 EXCEPT†)

TITLE	PRICE	TITLE	PRICE	TITLE	PRICE
COMPLETE FAMILY COOKBOOK*†	3.95	FAMILY DESSERT COOKBOOK	2.25	GARDEN COOKBOOK	1.95
SOPHIE KAY'S COOKBOOK†	2.50	GOURMET ON THE GO	2.25	WHOLE GRAIN COOKBOOK	1.95
NATURALLY NUTRITIOUS	2.25	IDEALS COOKIE COOKBOOK	1.95	FROM MAMA'S KITCHEN	1.95
FESTIVE PARTY COOKBOOK	2.25	SIMPLY DELICIOUS	2.25	OUTDOOR COOKBOOK	1.95
SOUPS FOR ALL SEASONS	2.25	MENUS FROM AROUND THE WORLD	1.95		
JUNIOR CHEF COOKBOOK	2.25	QUICK & SIMPLE COOKING FOR TWO	1.95	**NEW BOOKLET OF RECIPE CARDS #1**	1.00
ALL HOLIDAYS COOKBOOK	2.25	AMERICAN COOKBOOK	1.95	**NEW BOOKLET OF RECIPE CARDS #2**	1.00
COUNTRY KITCHEN	2.25	FAMILY COOKBOOK I	2.25	**COOKBOOK VIEWER (CLEAR LUCITE)**	4.00

SOFT COVER BOOKS 8½ x 11, B = 5¾ x 7¼, C = 4⅛ x 7 PAPERBACK

TITLE		PRICE	TITLE	PRICE	TITLE		PRICE
HAYMOW HERITAGE		3.75	VEGETABLE GARDENING		**HAPPY BIRTHDAY**		1.50
CREATIVE CRAFTS #1		2.95	MADE EASY	2.50	**HAPPY VALENTINE'S DAY**		1.50
LET'S HAVE A PARTY (FEB)		2.75	A GARDEN OF THOUGHTS	2.25	FAITH FOR TODAY		1.50
TO GOD BE THE GLORY		2.75	FUN WITH HANGING PLANTS	2.25	**CHEERFUL THOUGHTS AT DAWN**	C	1.50
LET'S WRAP IT UP		2.75	DOWN TO EARTH HOUSEPLANTS	2.25	HAPPINESS IS A FRIEND LIKE YOU		1.50
THIS IS OUR LAND		2.50	GOD BLESS AMERICA	2.25	THOUGHTS FOR EVERY DAY	C	1.50
BIRD WATCHER'S HANDBOOK	B	2.50	CRAFTS FOR EVERYONE	1.95	GET WELL WISHES		1.50
			MESSAGES OF CHRISTIAN FAITH	C 1.50			

SPECIAL CHILDREN'S BOOKS (SOFT COVER) 8½ x 11 *HARDBOUND

TITLE	PRICE	TITLE	PRICE	TITLE	PRICE
ONCE UPON A RHYME* (MAR)	3.95	**DOWN EASTER BUNNY LANE**	1.50	ZIGGY AND HIS MUSIC	1.25
STORIES CHILDREN LOVE*	3.50	STORIES FOR A RAINY DAY	1.25	ZIGGY AND WHAT ANIMALS SAY	1.25
STORYBOOK FAVORITES *	3.00	FUN & GAMES FOR CHILDREN	1.25		
THE CIRCUS	1.75	ZIGGY AND HIS COLORS	1.25		

DAYSTAR GREETING CARDS—PACK OF 12 (1 OF EACH DESIGN) $5.00 (NO SINGLE CARD ORDERS)

STATIONERY PORTFOLIO @ $1.00

NOTES BY IDEALS 4 x 5 @ $1.25—*1.50 (SPECIAL Purchase any 4 box sets deduct $.50)

	SET 1	SET 12	SET 22	SET 30		SET 40*	SET 44*	SET 48*
		SET 19	SET 24	VARIETY	SET 36	SET 41*	SET 45*	SET 49*
		SET 20		SET 33		SET 42*	SET 46*	SET 50*
	SET 10	SET 21	SET 28	SET 34	SET 39	SET 43*	SET 47*	SET 51*

TOTAL _____

POSTAGE AND HANDLING _____

SUB. TOTAL _____

WIS. RES. ONLY ADD 4% TAX (NOT ON SUBS.) _____

TOTAL DUE _____

SEE OTHER SIDE FOR BOOKLETS & TO ENTER ADDITIONAL SUBSCRIPTIONS

SEAL WELL AND MAIL
Check or Money Orders May Be Enclosed with Safety
*YOUR ZIP CODE IS NECESSARY

DISTINCTIVE GREETING BOOKLETS @ .75 EA (5⅜ x 7¼) MINIMUM ORDER 3—BUY 10 OR MORE DEDUCT $1.00

VALENTINE	TO A DEAR FRIEND	BABY'S HERE
EASTER	FRIENDSHIP	BIRTHDAY GREETINGS
GRADUATION WISHES	SINCERE SYMPATHY	BIRTHDAY WISHES (MAR)
TO THE BRIDE	IN SYMPATHY	ON YOUR BIRTHDAY
CONGRATULATIONS ON YOUR WEDDING	TO COMFORT YOU	BOUQUET OF WELL WISHES
HAPPY FATHER'S DAY	HAVE FAITH IN GOD	MAY YOU SOON FEEL BETTER
MOTHERS DAY (MAR)	THANK YOU	THROUGH THE KITCHEN DOOR
FOR MOTHER	HAPPY ANNIVERSARY	MAY ALL YOUR DREAMS COME TRUE
CONGRATULATIONS MOM & DAD	A HAPPY ANNIVERSARY	

87

THANK YOU!

FOLD HERE FIRST

☐ IF YOU WISH TO RECEIVE OUR IDEALS CATALOG CHECK HERE. ENTER FRIEND'S NAMES UNDER SPACE PROVIDED OR SEPARATE SHEET.

☐ SEND FUND RAISING INFORMATION

☐ SEND BUSINESS GIFT INFORMATION

87

FOLD SIDE FLAPS FIRST — THEN FOLD HERE

Wisconsin Residents Please Note:
You must Add 4% sales tax on all products sent to Wisconsin addresses, except bimonthly IDEALS issues and subscriptions to IDEALS bimonthly issues.

FOLD SIDE FLAPS FIRST

When properly sealed with the above gummed flap this envelope and its contents will travel safely through the mail.

ideals PUBLISHING CORP.

11315 WATERTOWN PLANK RD.
MILWAUKEE, WISCONSIN 53201

ZIP CODE

( )

from

FOR OFFICE USE ONLY

ENTRD		TYPE	KEY	AMT
REMTC		IDEALS	1	
K	MO	CA	CS	2	
CHECK FOR ACCURACY		CKBKS	3	
		OTHER	4	
OVER PAY		GRTS	5	
		BINDERS	8	
		FREIGHT	9	
		SUB-ID	11	
		SUB-CS	12	
INVOICE AMT		TAX	13	
		POSTAGE	14	

FOLD HERE FIRST

IDENTIFY AS A
GIFT FROM_____

TO_____

ADDRESS_____

CITY_____ STATE_____ ZIP_____

MAIL DATE & OCCASION_____

QTY	TITLE	PRICE
	*1 Yr. Subscription (6 issues) to IDEALS	$10.00
	*2 Yr. Subscription (12 issues) to IDEALS	$17.00
	*3 Yr. Subscription (18 issues) to IDEALS	$24.00
	Quarterly Country Scene Subscription (4 seasonal issues) Begin with Country Scene **VOLUME #** ☐ **ISSUE #** ☐	$ 7.50
	LIST OTHER GIFT SELECTIONS BELOW	
SEND CATALOG ☐		

IDENTIFY AS A
GIFT FROM_____

TO_____

ADDRESS_____

CITY_____ STATE_____ ZIP_____

MAIL DATE & OCCASION_____

QTY	TITLE	PRICE
	*1 Yr. Subscription (6 issues) to IDEALS	$10.00
	*2 Yr. Subscription (12 issues) to IDEALS	$17.00
	*3 Yr. Subscription (18 isssues) to IDEALS	$24.00
	Quarterly Country Scene Subscription (4 seasonal issues) Begin with Country Scene **VOLUME #** ☐ **ISSUE #** ☐	$ 7.50
	LIST OTHER GIFT SELECTIONS BELOW	
SEND CATALOG ☐		

NOTE.....*Your Gift Subscription will begin with **FIRESIDE** unless otherwise indicated.

Start my **Gift Subscription** with_____